What's Your Sound HOUND the HOUND?

by
MO WILLEMS

Balzer + Bray
An Imprint of HarperCollins*Publishers*

What's your sound Hound the Hound?

What's your sound Chick the Chick?

What's your sound Cow the Cow?

What's your sound Bunny the Bunny?

Sounds like . . .

somebody
needs a hug!

To Trixie, who can make

all kinds of sounds

Balzer + Bray is an imprint of HarperCollins Publishers.

What's Your Sound, Hound the Hound? Copyright © 2010 by Mo Willems Manufactured in China.
All rights reserved. No part of this book may be used or reproduced in any manner whatsoever
without written permission except in the case of brief quotations embodied in critical articles
and reviews. For information address HarperCollins Children's Books, a division of HarperCollins
Publishers, 195 Broadway, New York, NY 10007.
www.harpercollinschildrens.com

Library of Congress Cataloging-in-Publication Data
Willems, Mo.
    What's your sound, Hound the Hound? : a Cat the Cat book / by Mo Willems. — 1st ed.
        p.   cm.
    Summary: Cat the Cat's animal friends make many different sounds.
    ISBN 978-0-06-172844-0 (trade bdg.) — ISBN 978-0-06-172845-7 (lib. bdg.)
    [1. Animal sounds—Fiction.] I. Title. II. Title: What is your sound, Hound the Hound?
PZ7.W65535Wh   2010   2009014410
[E]—dc22   CIP
                                                                                       AC

Typography by Martha Rago
17   18   SCP   10 9 8 7 6 5 4
❖
First Edition